Hey Jack!

The Worry Monsters

By Sally Rippin

Illustrated by Stephanie Spartels

hardie grant EGMONT

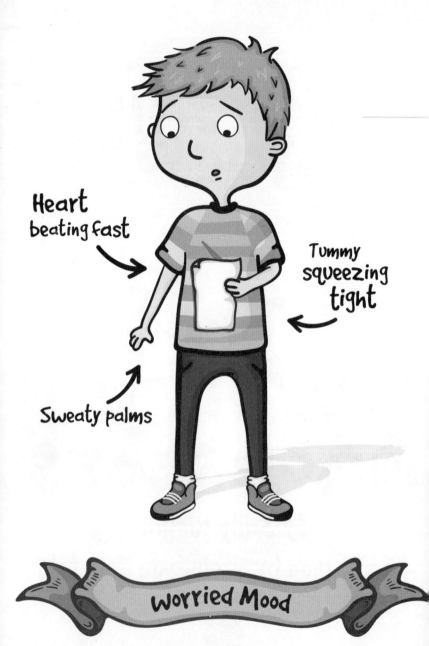

Chapter One

This is Jack.

Today Jack is feeling worried. His class has a spelling test next week.

Jack is good at maths and art, but terrible at spelling. He can't understand why *to*, *too* and *two* are all spelt differently. Spelling makes no sense!

Jack has 24 words to remember.

Outside it is **sunny** and Jack's puppy wants to play. Jack pushes the list of words to the bottom of his bag. He will worry about the spelling test later.

Jack and Scraps play outside in the back garden. They laugh and **bark** and roll around on the grass.

Soon it is time to go inside for dinner. Jack's mum has cooked his favourite – pasta bake!

She gives him an extra big serving.

'Did you get any school notices today?' Jack's mum asks.

Suddenly Jack remembers the list of words at the bottom of his bag.

His tummy squeezes
tight. He looks down
at his plate.

'Um… no,' he says.

Jack doesn't want
to think about the
spelling test. It makes
his tummy **hurt**.
He tries to finish his
dinner, but the pasta
doesn't taste so good
anymore.

That night, Jack lies

awake in the dark.

The worries in

his tummy are getting

bigger and bigger.

They feel like

big scary monsters

that are whispering

mean things to him.

Jack turns on the light.

He gets out of bed and

goes to his school bag.

The list of words is

still **scrunched**

up at the bottom.

But then Jack sees the

comic book he got

from the school library.

Jack snuggles back
into bed with the
comic book.

There is still a

whole week until

the test. He will worry

about it tomorrow.

Chapter Two

All that week Jack

is very busy. At school

he plays soccer with

his friend Billie.

After school he plays
with Scraps.

On the weekend he
and Billie build a
huge pirate ship from
chairs and broomsticks
and bed sheets.

On Sunday night
Jack packs his bag
for school.

15

At the bottom of

the bag is a scrunched

up piece of paper.

Oh no! The spelling test.

Jack has forgotten to

practise his words.

And the test is tomorrow!

Jack feels his tummy

shrink with worry.

He pulls out the test

and looks at it.

There are so many

tricky words on there.

Jack knows he will get
them all wrong. He stuffs
it back into his bag
and crawls into bed.

That night he imagines
the worry monsters
in his room again.
This time they are
even bigger and
scarier than before.

The next morning Jack
feels sick in his tummy.

He doesn't want to
go to school.

He wants to tell his
mum about the test.
But he is worried that
she will be **cross**
with him.

Jack walks to school
with Billie and her mum.
He is very quiet.

'Is something wrong?'
Billie asks.

'No,' says Jack,
shaking his head.

'Are you sure?' says Billie.

'I'm fine,' says Jack

crossly. He wishes Billie

would stop asking.

In class, Jack's tummy
ache starts to **hurt**
even more.

'I don't feel well,'
Jack says to Billie.

Billie puts up her hand.
'Ms Walton,' she says.
'Jack doesn't feel well.
Can I take him
to sick bay?'

'Oh dear,' Ms Walton says.

'You do look a little

pale, Jack.'

'Billie will take

you to sick bay.

I'll call your parents.

You'll miss the

spelling test, but you

can do it tomorrow.'

Jack lies in sick bay

waiting to be picked up.

Billie waits with him.

'Can I tell you
something?' Jack says.

'Sure,' says Billie.
'What is it?'

'I didn't practise my
spelling words,' Jack says.
'I don't know what
to tell Mum and Dad.'

'Just tell them
the truth,' Billie says.

Jack lies back. There are
patterns on the ceiling
that remind him of
the worry monsters.
He closes his eyes
to make them go away.

Chapter Three

At home, Jack's dad

tucks him into bed.

He puts a cold washcloth

on Jack's forehead.

'So,' his dad says kindly.

'Do you want to tell me
what's wrong?'

Jack hangs his head.

'I had a spelling test today,' he says. 'I forgot to practise the words.'

'You forgot?' says his dad. He lifts his eyebrows and **smiles**.

Jack sighs. 'I'm terrible at spelling, Dad,' he says in a little voice. 'I just can't do it!'

'That doesn't sound like my Jack,' his dad says.
He gives Jack a cuddle.
'Why don't we practise the words together?'

'You will have to go
back to school sometime,
and the spelling test
will still be there.'

Jack climbs out of
bed. He pulls the
wrinkled paper
from his school bag
and hands it to his dad.

His dad reads the words.

'Hmm. Some of these are

tricky,' he says. 'But I have

an idea. Come and help

me with some cooking.'

Jack looks surprised.

'But I thought we

were going to practise

my spelling?' he says.

'We are!' says his dad.

Jack follows his dad
into the kitchen.

'Right,' says his dad.
'First course is
alphabet soup.
Then words on
bread and biscuits
shaped like letters.

We are going to
practise those words,
then eat them up when
we get them right.'

Jack laughs. This sounds
like **fun**!

All afternoon Jack and
his dad make words
out of biscuits, pasta
and even cut-up fruit.

When they have
eaten all the food,
Jack and his dad
practise with a pencil
and paper. Soon Jack
knows all the words
off by heart. He can't
wait to do the test
tomorrow!

That night, Jack lies

in bed and waits for

the worry monsters to

come. When they do, he

is **ready** for them.

'Go away!' he says.

'I've practised

my words for the

spelling test.'

The worry monsters disappear.

Jack knows they will come back again someday. But he also knows that he doesn't need to be **afraid** of them anymore.

When Jack does his test the next day, Ms Walton is very surprised.

'My goodness, Jack!' she says. 'You have improved. Well done!'

'Wow!' Billie says when she sees his mark. 'How did you remember all those words?'

'I'll teach you a trick
my dad taught me,'
Jack grins. 'But I hope
you like alphabet soup!'

Hey Jack! The Crazy Cousins By Sally Rippin

Hey Jack! The Scary Solo By Sally Rippin

Hey Jack! The Winning Goal By Sally Rippin

Hey Jack! The Robot Blues By Sally Rippin

Hey Jack! The Worry Monsters By Sally Rippin

Hey Jack! The New Friend By Sally Rippin

Hey Jack! The Worst Sleepover By Sally Rippin

Hey Jack! The Lost Reindeer By Sally Rippin

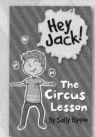

Hey Jack! The Circus Lesson By Sally Rippin

Hey Jack! The Bumpy Ride By Sally Rippin

Hey Jack! The Top Team By Sally Rippin

Hey Jack! The Playground Problem By Sally Rippin

Hey Jack! The Best Party Ever By Sally Rippin

Hey Jack! The Big Adventure By Sally Rippin

Hey Jack! The Bravest Kid By Sally Rippin

Hey Jack! The Toy Sale By Sally Rippin

Hey Jack! The Other Teacher By Sally Rippin

Hey Jack! The Party Invite By Sally Rippin

Hey Jack! The Extra-special Group By Sally Rippin

Hey Jack! The Star of the Week By Sally Rippin